W9-BBC-955

Mammoth and Me

Written and illustrated by Alex Craig Hall

One night
there was
a knock at
our front door.

I opened it and there
he stood – Mammoth.
As big as the biggest truck
and hairier than a yak.

Mammoth had been woken
from a many-thousand-
year slumber by the
rumbling and grumbling
of his hungry belly.

Mammoth was much too big to get in our front door.

He put his trunk through the window and I fed him fish sticks and peas, straight from the freezer.

He slept in the
garden.

But he flattened Dad's shed.

Dad said,
"That mammoth can't stay here."

"Come on," I said to Mammoth.
"Let's go to the park."

But he squashed
the swing . . .

and the
climbing frame . . .

and the see-saw.

So we left and went to the pool.

But when Mammoth dived in,
the swimming pool turned
into one great big splash.

All that water gave him a tummy ache. He had an accident – all over a car! The driver was pretty upset. He said, "This town is no place for a mammoth. He'll have to go!"

I didn't want Mammoth
to leave. I loved him.
But what could I do?

Then we saw a bus.
It had broken down.

"How will I get everyone home?"
said the bus driver.
Then Mammoth had an idea.

Mammoth carried everyone home.

Now the whole town wanted
to be Mammoth's friend.

The very best part was,
Dad said Mammoth
could live with us after all!

For Gilbert
Algy Craig Hall

First American edition published in 2012 by Boxer Books Limited.

First published in Great Britain in 2012
by Boxer Books Limited.
www.boxerbooks.com

Text and illustrations copyright © 2012 Algy Craig Hall

The illustrations were prepared using watercolour paints, pencil and graphite stick.
The text is set in Adobe Caslon.

ISBN 978-1-907967-22-1

1 3 5 7 9 10 8 6 4 2

Printed in China

All of our papers are sourced from managed forests and renewable resources.